A FRIENDSHIP YARN

Lisa Moser

illustrated by
Olga Demidova

Albert Whitman & Company
Chicago, Illinois

For my dear friend Sara Akin,
who is loving and gracious and would
always share her yarn.—LM

To all friendship knitters—OD

Library of Congress Cataloging-in-Publication data is on file with the publisher.

First published in the United States of America in 2019 by Albert Whitman & Company
ISBN 978-0-8075-0762-9 (hardcover)
ISBN 978-0-8075-0761-2 (ebook)

Printed in China
10 9 8 7 6 5 4 3 2 1 HH 24 23 22 21 20 19

Design by Ellen Kokontis

For more information about Albert Whitman & Company,
visit our website at www.albertwhitman.com.

100 Years of Albert Whitman & Company
Celebrate with us in 2019!

Badger and Porcupine met under the walnut tree and shared a pot of tea like they did every morning. As the day warmed up, Porcupine helped Badger rake leaves, and Badger helped Porcupine stir a big pot of apple butter.

Badger sniffed the air. “Winter weather is coming.”

“That’s a cold cup of tea,” sighed Porcupine. “I’ll have to gather firewood. This is my last log.”

“Don’t worry,” said Badger. “I’ll help you.”

“You are such a dear friend,” said Porcupine.

The two friends walked into the woods to gather logs. Porcupine took the high trail. Badger took the low one.

A peddler's cart jinglejangled down the road.

A ball of yarn tumbled out

and unrolled

and unrolled

and unrolled

until a bright-colored string of yarn stretched out the length of the woods.

Porcupine picked up one end of the yarn. Far away, Badger picked up the other end of the yarn.

"Come back," called Badger.

"You lost your yarn," called Porcupine.

"Keep it," said the peddler, waving merrily. "Don't have time to stop."

Badger looked at the yarn. "I can pick up logs later. I'll use this yarn to knit a backpack for picnics with Porcupine." Badger ran home, jumped over her pile of books, and dove under her bed for her knitting needles.

Porcupine looked at her yarn. "Well, fill my sugar bowl. Who needs logs? This is exactly what I need to make a lovely tablecloth for tea time with Badger." She dashed home and pulled her knitting needles out of her tidy sewing basket.

Clickety-click, snickety-snick went Badger's needles.

But when she had only three stitches to go, the whole thing unraveled...

Floop.

Floop.

Floop-floop-floop.

Clickety-click, snickety-snick went Porcupine's needles.

But when she had only three stitches to go, the whole thing unraveled…

Floop.

Floop.

Floop-floop-floop.

Porcupine followed the yarn to Badger's house. "I think you have my yarn," said Porcupine.

"This is my yarn," said Badger. "The peddler gave it to me."

"Well, flatten my cake! You're wrong," said Porcupine. "The peddler gave it to *me*!" She stomped back to her house.

"Cookie crumbles," said Porcupine. "I'll make something for myself—a tail for my kite."

Clickety-click, snickety-snick.

Floop.

Floop.

Floop-floop-floop.

“Ooh, a rain cloud,” said Badger.
“I’ll knit a hat to keep warm and dry.
Too bad for Porcupine.”

Clickety-click, snickety-snick.

Floop.

Floop.

Floop-floop-floop.

“A net to catch walnuts,” said Porcupine. “And I won’t share any.”

Clickety-click, snickety-snick.

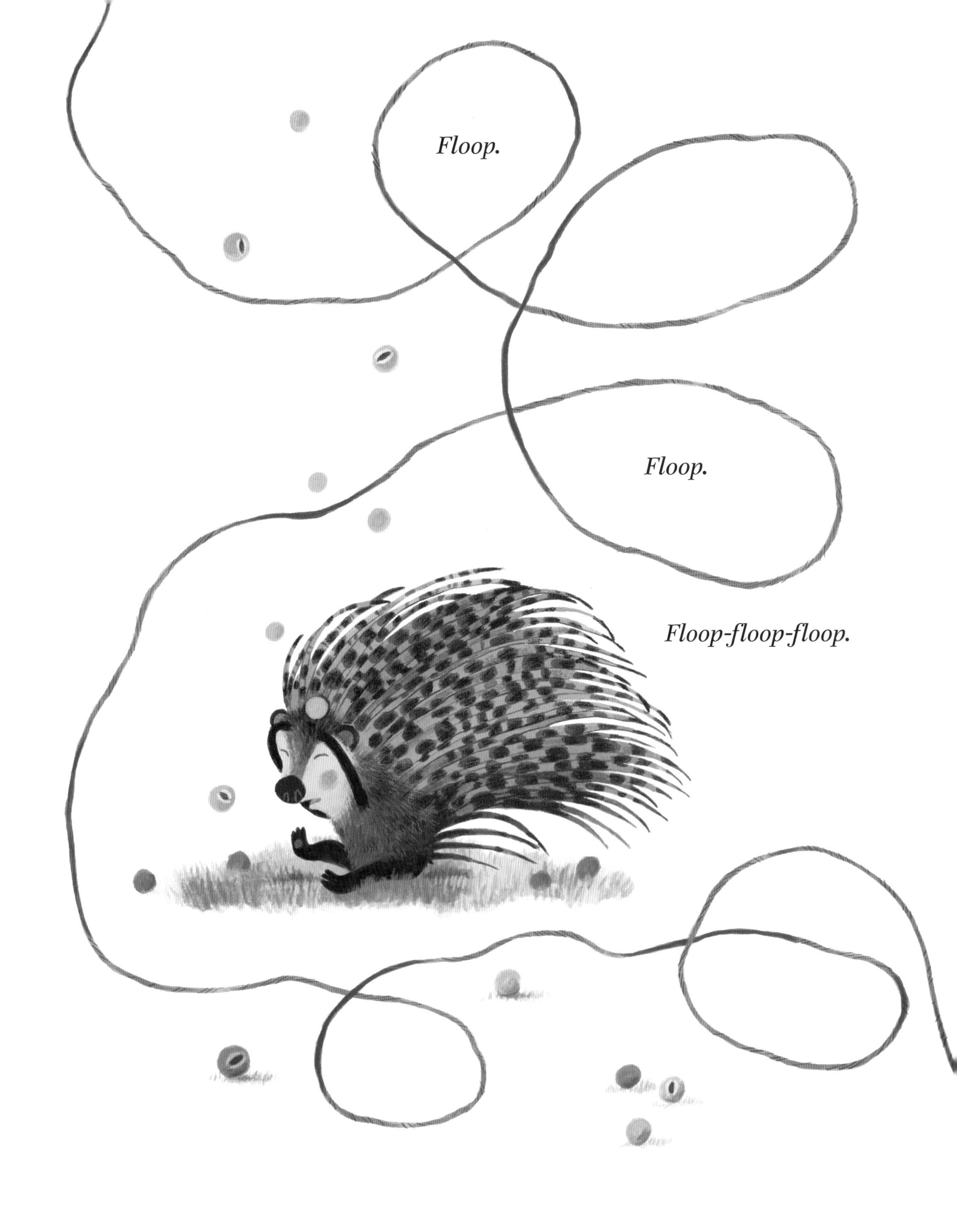
Floop.
Floop.
Floop-floop-floop.

"A hammock for me, me,
and just me," said Badger.

Clickety-click, snickety-snick.

Floop.

Floop.

Floop-floop-floop.

"A tent to hide in," said Porcupine,
"so I never have to see Badger again!"
Clickety-click, snickety-snick.

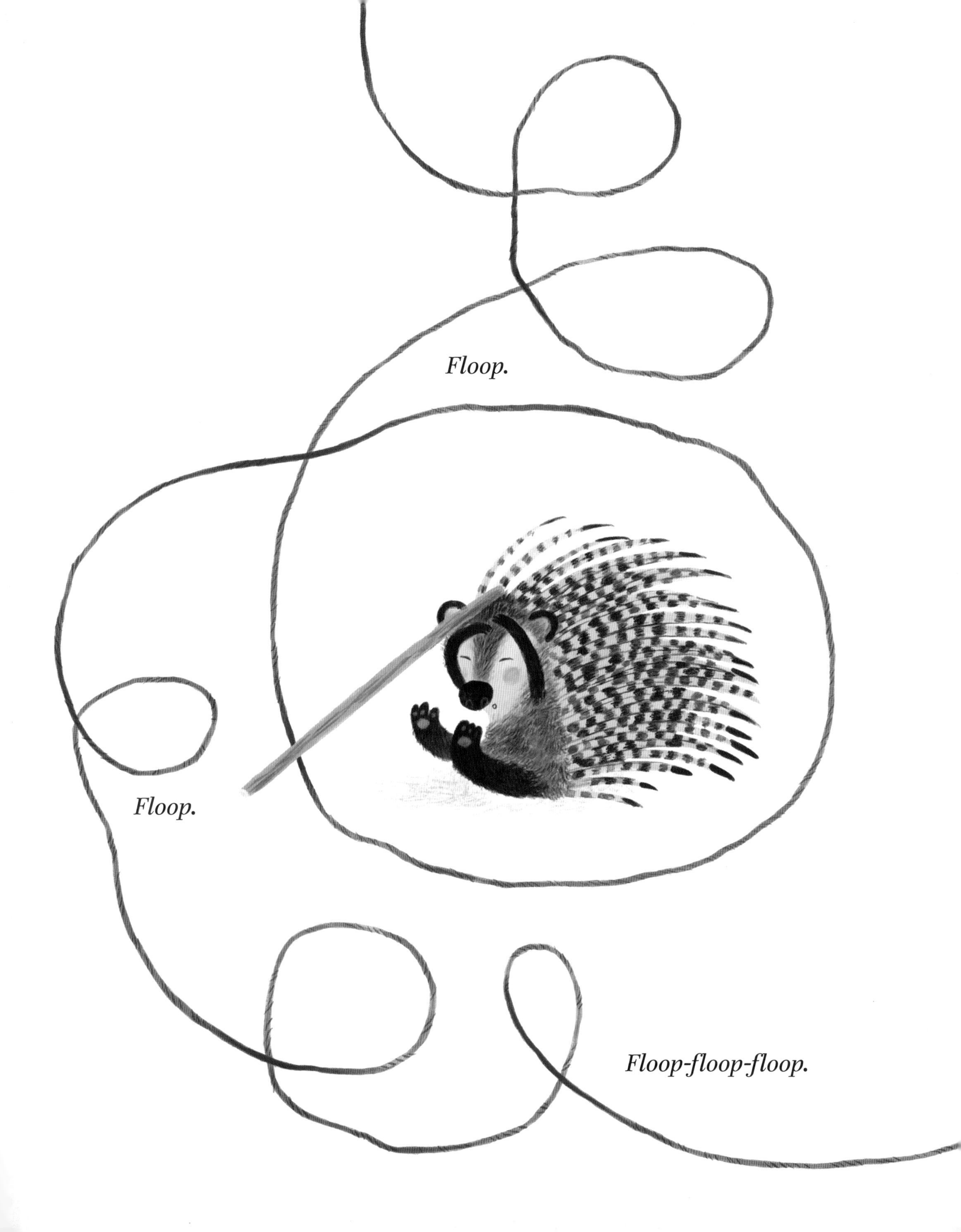

Floop.

Floop.

Floop-floop-floop.

“A sail for my boat,” said Badger, “so I can sail far, far away from Porcupine!”

Clickety-click, snickety-snick.

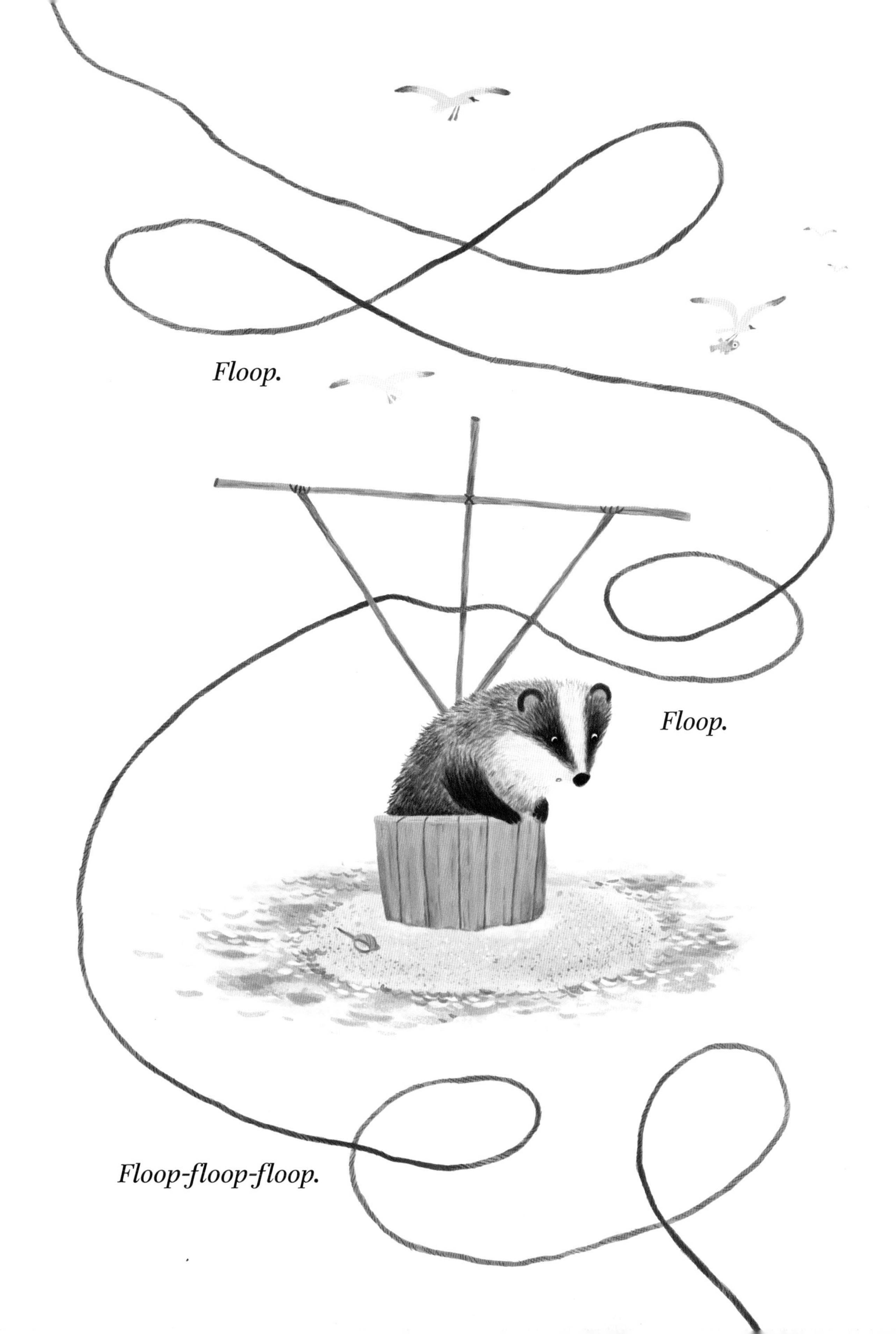

Floop.

Floop.

Floop-floop-floop.

Badger pounded on Porcupine's door. "Give me back my yarn!"

"It's mine!" cried Porcupine.

"Mine!" yelled Badger.

"You're not my friend anymore," said Porcupine.

"I don't want to be your friend! And I don't want to be your neighbor!" said Badger.

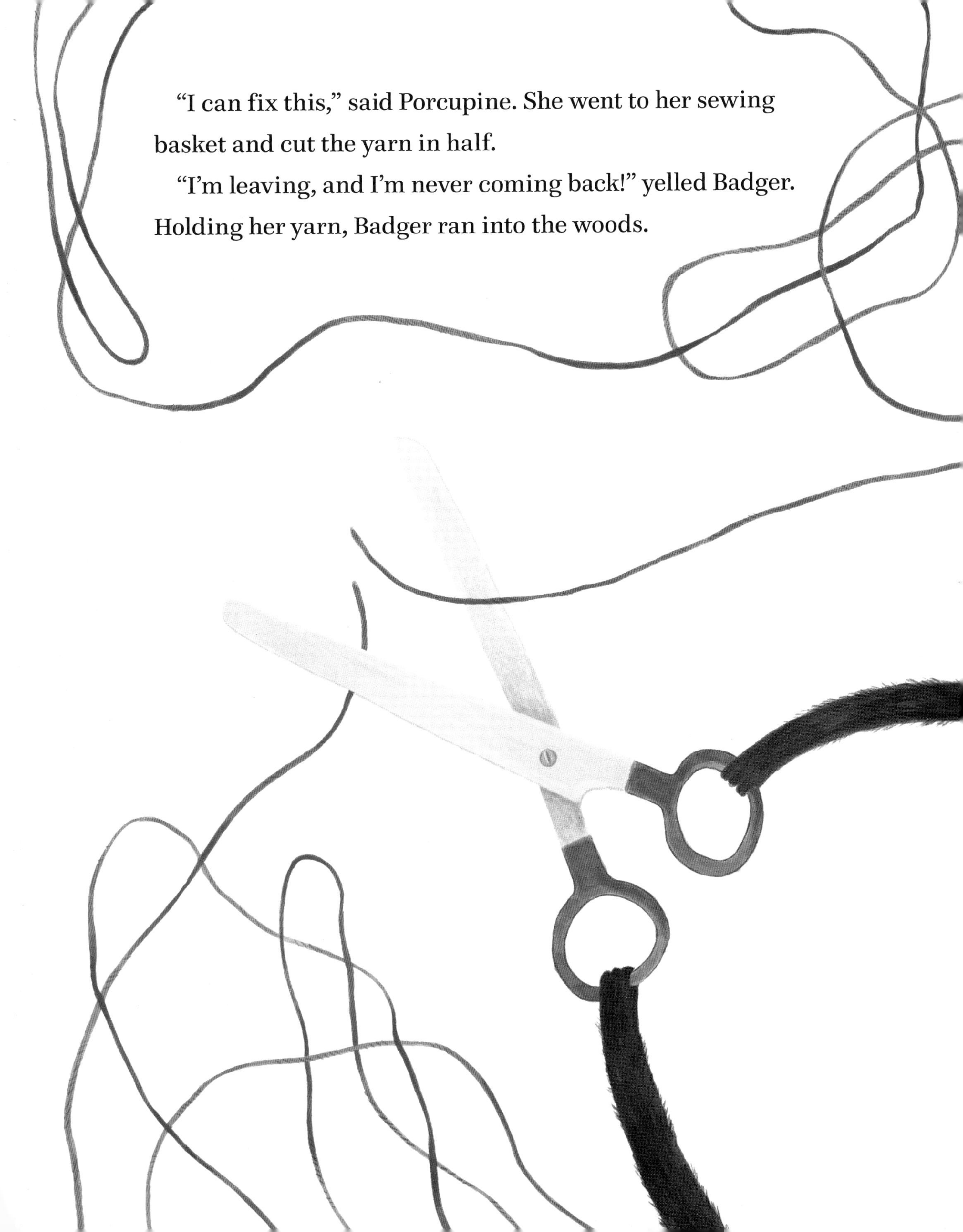

“I can fix this,” said Porcupine. She went to her sewing basket and cut the yarn in half.

“I’m leaving, and I’m never coming back!” yelled Badger. Holding her yarn, Badger ran into the woods.

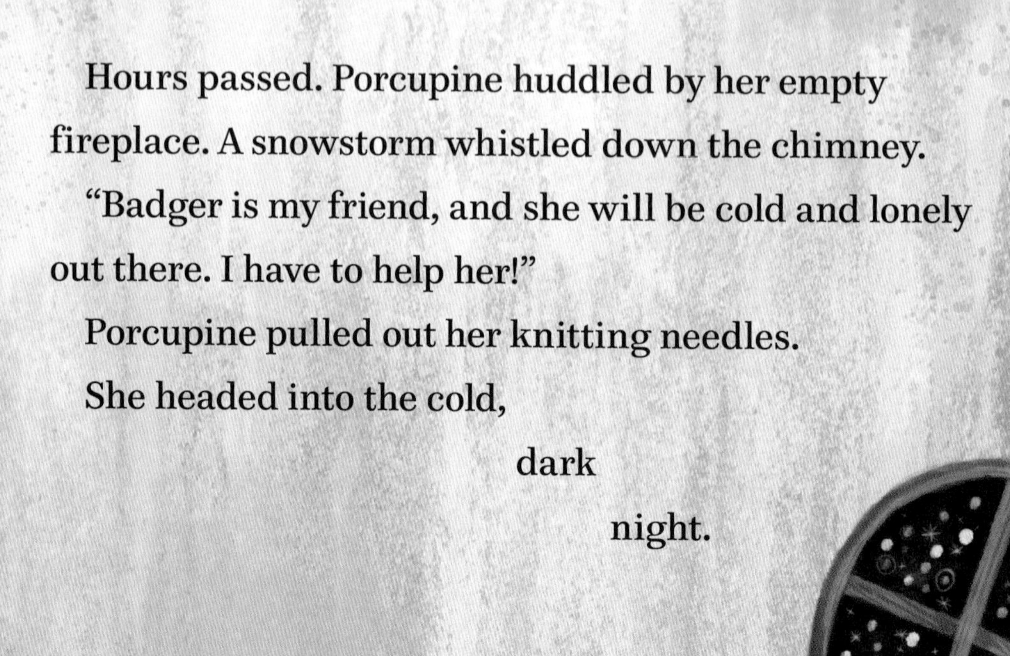

Hours passed. Porcupine huddled by her empty fireplace. A snowstorm whistled down the chimney.

"Badger is my friend, and she will be cold and lonely out there. I have to help her!"

Porcupine pulled out her knitting needles.

She headed into the cold,

dark

night.

Badger hunkered down in an old log and worried. “It’s getting colder every minute, and Porcupine is out of firewood. She’ll be freezing. She’s my friend. I have to help her!”

Badger pulled out her knitting needles.

She headed into the cold,

dark

night.

Clickety. Clickety.
Snickety. Snickety.

Click.
Snick.

Oof!

Porcupine and Badger ran straight into each other.

"Well, polish my silver!" said Porcupine. "I found you! You're safe! Put on this sweater I knit for you."

"Quick," said Badger. "It's freezing out here. Put on this sweater I knit for you."

Porcupine and Badger
admired their new sweaters.

"I'm sorry we fought,"
said Porcupine.

"Me too," said Badger.

"Will you come over for toast and apple butter?" asked Porcupine.

"Love to," said Badger, picking up a bunch of logs. "You're going to need these."

The two friends headed home together into the night that didn't feel

so very cold

or very dark,

after all.